Grégoire Solotareff

You Big and Me Small

FIREFLY BOOKS

Once upon a time, there was a little elephant.

And there was the king of animals.

The king wasn't very little, but he wasn't very big either.

One day the little elephant, who had lost his parents,
followed the lion all the way to his palace,
but the lion wouldn't let him in.
"Go away!" he said. "Disappear, you dirty rascal!
Turn around and go! Leave me alone!"
But the lion was acting more out of irritation than meanness.

When the lion went to bed,
the little elephant stayed outside the palace doors,
and he fell asleep without saying a word
or shedding a tear, because he was very brave.

Also, he also had nothing else to do and, more importantly,
had no one else in the world.

The next morning it was especially cold, and the lion felt a touch of sadness when he saw the little elephant sleeping outdoors on the ground.

The lion invited the elephant into his palace and offered him breakfast.
"Come on, come in!" he told him, "Eat something. I don't want to see you die of hunger or freeze to death!"

That same night the king read him stories —
tales of fierce and invincible lions.
The little elephant didn't take his eyes off the king.
He wasn't exactly afraid of him, not really . . .
Well, he was maybe a little afraid,
but mostly he admired the lion.

"You can speak, I hope?" asked the lion.
"I haven't even heard the sound of your voice yet."
"Me small!" said the elephant.
"I see . . . " sighed the lion.

It's true that the little elephant didn't know how to speak well
(or how to read or write, of course), but he knew how to sing
little songs that his mother had taught him.

That night he slept in the palace, stretched out besides the royal bed, and he softly sang one of his little songs to put the lion to sleep. He put himself to sleep, too.

After a few days, they spent every moment together.
For hours at a time, the lion told the little elephant
about everything he knew, everything he'd seen,
everything he'd read, all of the trips he'd taken,
and even the trips he hadn't taken but had always
wanted to take.
The lion talked about terrible animals he'd fought,
about a lion princess he knew, and about his throne, his crown
and, finally, about everything he owns,
and he owns a lot of things, since he's the king of animals.

"You big!" said the little elephant.
They thereby became inseparable,
like brothers: one big and one little.
Or maybe like a son and his father,
which isn't exactly the same thing.

One afternoon, while everyone else was napping,
the lion dressed up like a dog, with a collar and leash,
to entertain the elephant.
But the lion quickly tired of this game.
"That's enough!" he said. "I'm still the king!
And we must go back in. It's getting cold."

On another day, the king put the elephant up on his shoulders,
and it's fantastic to be on the shoulders of a lion,
when you're an elephant.
"Get down, now!" said the lion abruptly.
The little elephant was really enjoying himself,
but he got down, of course, without grumbling.

On yet another day, the king wanted to play King of Kings:
The little elephant had to do everything —
absolutely everything! — the lion told him to do,
and he could not refuse.
That game went on for hours and hours,
and the lion never tired of it. When the little elephant asked,
"And now what should we do?"
The king answered, "Well, now we keep playing."

Time passed and the elephant grew larger, like all children do!
He learned how to speak, and he learned how to do lots of
other things too.

As for the lion, he didn't grow. Like a dad, he had finished growing a long time ago. "You are huge," said the king one day. "Am I?" answered the elephant.

"Something isn't right!" said the king.
"You're too big for me!
When we walk together, I no longer feel like the king."
And so, to appear smaller,
the elephant would go down on all four legs,
and the lion would climb up on his back.
"For me," the elephant said to the king, "it doesn't change anything."
"Really?" asked the lion.
"Really, truly, definitely!" answered the elephant.
And he started singing a song he'd invented:

"You big and me small.
Even if you now seem small
Because I have grown so tall,
You'll always be the bigger one,
The most elegant one,
The king when all is said and done.

And me, I'm still small
But I can still have a ball.
I'll tell one and all:
You big and me small."

"You're right!" said the lion after hearing the song.
"Me big and you small, very small."
And they continued strolling all afternoon long.

"I've decided it's not going well!" said the lion after their walk.
"You are too big for me, and I have nothing left to teach you.
I've thought long and hard about it. You need to leave because
I no longer feel like the king."

After a long silence full of sadness, the elephant said, "Okay. You must have thought about it for a very long time before telling me. If that's really what you want, I'll leave." And so he left.

Many years later, the elephant still thought about the lion a lot
— at least once a day.

One day, while riding around in a taxi, the elephant saw
someone on the sidewalk who was covered with a blanket.
The elephant stopped the taxi and approached.
It was the lion!

"Hello, Your Majesty! Can I help you?" the elephant asked
timidly, since he wasn't sure if the king would remember him.
"Your Majesty?" the lion asked, stunned.
"Who is still addressing me this way? . . .
Wait, I recognize you! You're the little elephant I took in
and then chased away! Me big and you small!"

"You big and me small!" replied the elephant.
And they fell into each other's arms.
"What's happened to you?" asked the elephant.
"Oh!" said the lion. "I haven't been king for a long time.
Can you believe they chased me away, too?
It seems I was too proud! Arrogant, they said. What foolishness!"

"And that crown that you're wearing?" asked the elephant.
"Well, it's a fake crown," answered the king.
"They stole the real one from me.
I'm even too weak to get up and find food for myself,
not to mention defend myself! That's how things are for me,
you see! I'm slowly dying, here, in the street!"

"No! No! No!" cried the elephant.
"I won't accept it! To me, you're still the king!"

After less than ten days, the king had recovered.
To not appear too big, the elephant walked on all four legs,
like he had done before.
"Can you take off your crown?" asked the elephant.
"It's tickling my belly, and it's not needed.
I know very well who is the king!"

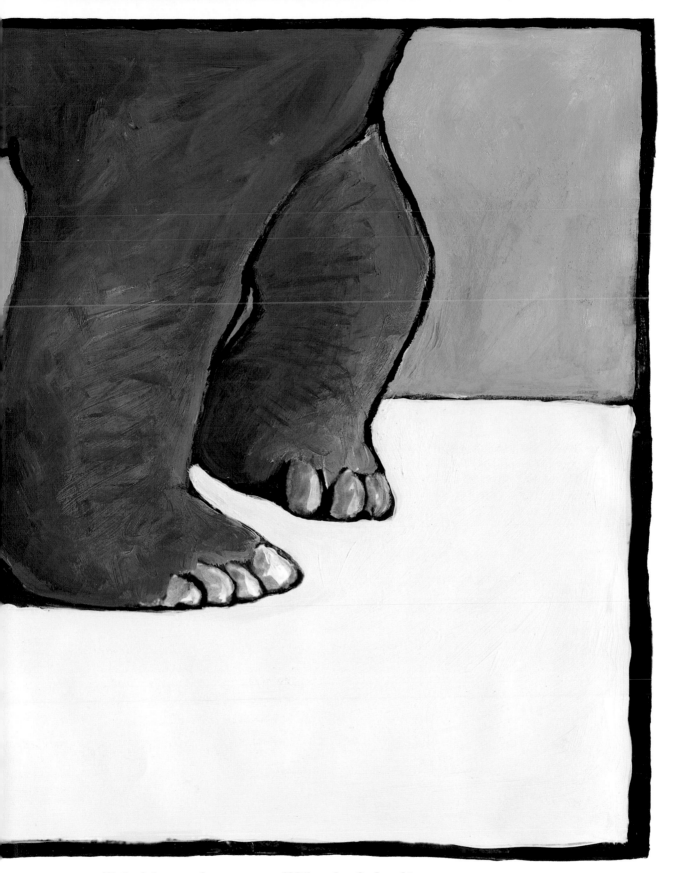

"Me big and you small?" asked the lion.
"You big and me small," answered the elephant.
"Now, we must go home. It's going to get dark soon."
"Let's go!" said the king. "I'll take off my crown at home."

A FIREFLY BOOK

Published by Firefly Books Ltd. 2017

First printing

Publisher Cataloging-in-Publication Data (U.S.)
Library of Congress Cataloging-in-Publication Data is available

Library and Archives Canada Cataloguing in Publication
Solotareff, Grégoire
[Toi grand et moi petit. English]
    You big and me small / Grégoire Solotareff.
Translation of: Toi grand et moi petit.
ISBN 978-0-228-10000-3 (hardcover)
    I. Title. II. Title: Toi grand et moi petit. English.
PZ7.S6962Yo 2017   j843'.914   C2017-901818-3

Published in the United States by
Firefly Books (U.S.) Inc.
P.O. Box 1338, Ellicott Station
Buffalo, New York 14205

Published in Canada by
Firefly Books Ltd.
50 Staples Avenue, Unit 1
Richmond Hill, Ontario L4B 0A7

Translator: Claudine Mersereau

Printed in China

 We acknowledge the financial support of the Government of Canada.